TRACEY CAMPBELL PEARSON

Where Does Joe Go?

Farrar Straus Giroux • New York

Distributed in Canada by Douglas & McIntyre Ltd.
Color separations by Hong Kong Scanner Arts
Printed and bound in the United States of America by Worzalla
Typography by G. Laurens
First edition, 1999

Library of Congress Cataloging-in-Publication Data
Pearson, Tracey Campbell.
    Where does Joe go? / Tracey Campbell Pearson. — 1st ed.
      p.   cm.
    Summary: Because Joe's Snack Bar always closes for the season,
the townspeople speculate about where Joe goes for the winter.
    ISBN 0-374-38319-7
    [1. Fast food restaurants—Fiction.   2. Restaurants—Fiction.
3. Santa Claus—Fiction.]   I. Title.
PZ7.P323318Wh 1999
[E]—dc21   98-37745

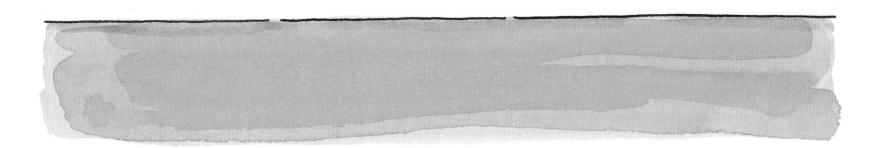

For Dennis

Every year, when winter is over and spring is finally here, Joe comes back to town.

Throughout the summer, crowds gather at Joe's

to eat hot dogs, creemees, and fries.

But after fall arrives, Joe disappears again, and

all winter long, everyone wonders: Where does Joe go?

"He's gone to the moon,"
cried tiny June.

"Or maybe the beach,"
said old Mr. Leach.

"I think he's on a cruise,"
said the woman buying shoes.

"He's having tea with the Queen," whispered Molly McLeen.

"He's digging for bones,"
said Oliver Jones.

"In Okefenokee!"
screamed Mrs. Bodoky.

Bird of the Week

Anhinga
34-36"

Floating Islands of Okefenokee

OKEFENOKEE SWAMP

"He's in the city,"
suggested Kitty.

"He's dancing the tango,"
said Mrs. Fandango.

"He's off to the pyramids,"
yelled all the Biddy kids.

"He's on a safari,"
said Charlie Maccari.

Then spring comes again, and the children call out,

"Joe, where have you been?"
But Joe won't tell a soul . . .